Wheezer's Story

by Wheezer the Squirrel

with Ann Southcombe

Wheezer's Story

Copyright ©2018 Ann Southcombe

All rights reserved.

Printed in the United States of America

No part of this book may be used or reproduced in any manner whatsoever without written permission, except in the case of brief quotations in articles and reviews.

Applegate Valley Publishing

info@applegatevalleypublishing.com

sulango@wildblue.net

For more information about Wheezer's Mom, visit www.atrans-specieslife.com

Design and production by

Deborah Perdue, Illumination Graphics, www.illuminationgraphics.com

Big Thanks to Deborah Perdue for donating her

time putting this together!

Mandala illustration by Jan Rice, www.etsy.com/shop/heartworks

Softcover: 978-0-9983677-7-4

Please know it is not a good idea to have a healthy squirrel as a pet.

In most states it is also illegal.

This book is dedicated to my writing teacher,

Tee Corinne, and all my friends who support my love

of squirrels, and of course, to my beloved Wheezer.

Wheezer wrote most of this book
His friend, Denise, gave him the toy squirrel
And I just took pictures while he played with it.
After printing the pictures, I saw the story!

Ann Southcombe

Hi, My name is Wheezer. I fell from my nest as an infant. Some passersby were kind enough to pick me up.

They took me to a wildlife rehabilitation center.

This is where my life was saved.

I was very sick the first four weeks and needed twenty four hour care. When I became a healthy two month old squirrel, it was discovered that I could never be returned to the forest. When I fell from my nest, I knocked my jaw crooked. My bottom teeth would grow into my nose if not trimmed every four weeks.

The human who raised me, took me home to live with her. She built a three story "squirrel condo" where I stay when she is not at home. Other wise, I am out playing around the house. I even get along with her five cats. I outsmart them all the time!

But I got lonely for squirrels.

One day my human brought home
"Peanut." She is not exactly like me
but close enough. Even though my
human is very intuitive with me,
she is just a hair shy of a squirrel.

Now I have someone to relate real squirrel
stuff to.

I told her my deepest squirrel secrets.

Then she told me hers.

She too had been lonely.

She was living in a store with other toys,

but no squirrels.

I could relate to that!

We shared squirrel food.

We played squirrel groom . . .

and tickle games for hours!

Soon we had to take a rest!

I asked if she would like to stay and live
with me.

Please stay.

She wasn't sure, which made me very sad.

I would share my favorite food.

Come, let me show you my condo.

Well,
what
do you
think?

She
said she
would
stay.
I am one
lucky
squirrel!

Even though I love my new friend,
the one I love the best
is my human, Ann!

This book is dedicated
to my dear Wheezer.
He passed away 4/21/05.
He will forever be in my heart.

I ♥
Wheezer
2002-4-22-05

Squirrels are in the top ten of intelligent animals.

Squirrels will adopt other squirrel babies if they are abandoned.

When a squirrel feels it is being watched, it may deceptively pretend to bury an object then hide the object in its mouth.

Only 15 to 25 percent of baby squirrels make it to their first birthday. so let them share your bird feeder or give them one of their own!

www.ingramcontent.com/pod-product-compliance
Lightning Source LLC
Chambersburg PA
CBHW041201100726
47911CB00016B/820